P9-DTB-077

THE LEGEND OF AUNTIE PO

THE LEGEND OF AUNTIE PO
SHING YIN KHOR
Kokila

KOKILA
An imprint of Penguin Random House LLC, New York

First published in the United States of America by Kokila,
an imprint of Penguin Random House LLC, 2021

Kokila & colophon are registered trademarks of Penguin Random House LLC.
Visit us online at penguinrandomhouse.com.
Library of Congress Cataloging-in-Publication Data is available.

Manufactured in China

ISBN 9780525554899 (PBK) 10 9 8 7 6 5 4 3 2 1
ISBN 9780525554882 (HC) 10 9 8 7 6 5 4 3 2 1

Design by Jasmin Rubero
Hand lettering by Shing Yin Khor

Heather L. Gilbraith assisted with pencils
Language consultant and translation by Chai Hiong Ng

The art for this book was created using digital pencils and hand-painted watercolor.

For my dad, who worked so I could paint.

CHAPTER ONE

This is a story about stories.
This is a story about gods and men.
The dinner bell is one of my jobs.
I have a lot of jobs.

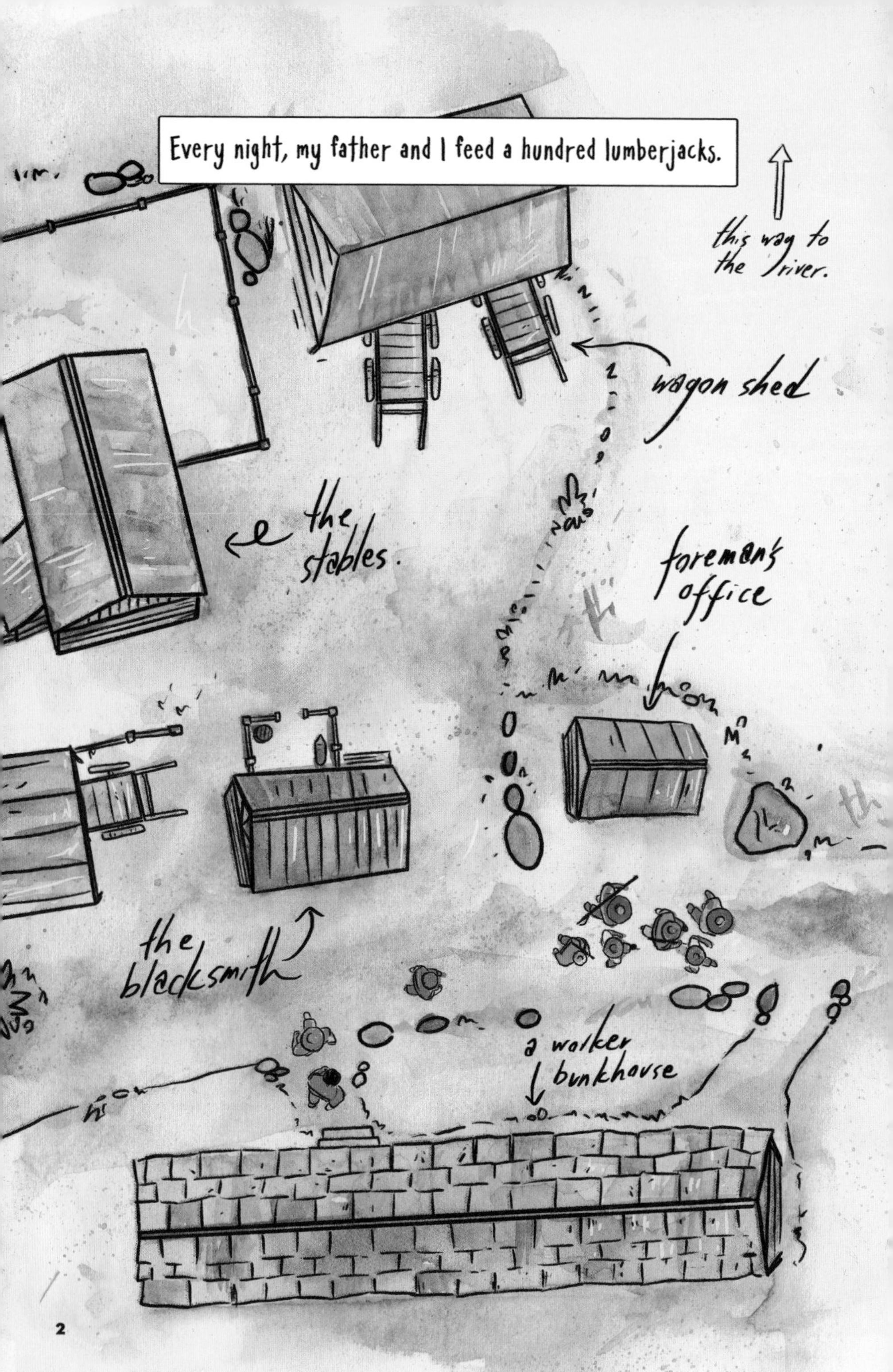

Every night, my father and I feed a hundred lumberjacks.

this way to the river.

wagon shed

the stables.

foreman's office

the blacksmith

a walker bunkhouse

We also feed forty Chinese workers who do not receive board.

I live here!

the kitchen

the school-house

Bee lives here.

My father has a little shrine in his cabin where he makes me pray every morning.
When I was little, he told me many stories of heroes and gods.
Every morning, he asks his parents for a blessing, asks for protection and prosperity for our little family.
My grandparents died before I met them. I don't know where home is.

I don't pray anymore. I inhale incense smoke and think of the things I have to do. Make the breakfasts. Assemble the lunch bags. Make dough. Peel potatoes. Make pie. We have a lot to do. We work a lot.
Went to town with Papa, back by dinner! (save me pie!) :B
My father doesn't tell stories anymore.

A logging camp in the Sierra Nevadas, 1885

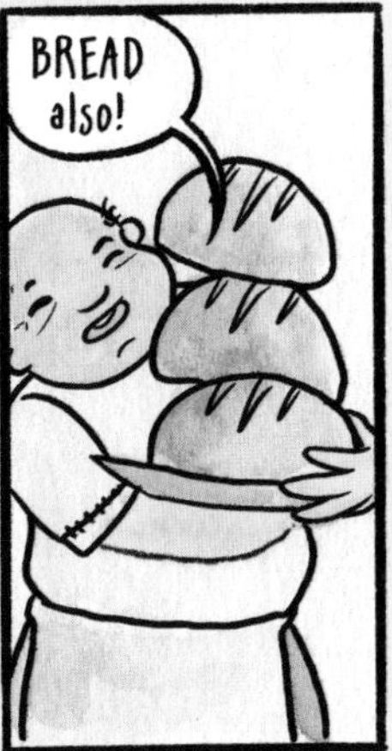

MORE POTATO!

Thank you, Mister Hao!

Thanks, boys!

Ha ha, thank you, boy...
Thank you also, ah boy...
I make the best pie for miles. Well, we're the only logging camp for at least forty miles.
Mei! Are the pies ready?
They're still cooling!

Please give us the pies! The men are about to riot.
Well, the men could learn some restraint. But please let us have the pies.
Ughhh...fine.
Thanks, Mei!

Mister Andersen runs the logging camp. He likes my pies the most.

吃饭
Dinner time!

Bee and I have been friends since we were little.

Pride and Prejudice!
This book belongs to
Hao Mei Lee
Thank you, Bee. You're so good at drawing.
Is there any pie left?
I've read it, you know.
You keep on borrowing my copy. I thought you'd want your own.
Chinese dinner's over! Let's go see about the pie!

Brought your plate back!
I also brought you a newspaper from town.
Well, I work for the company. It's the company's plate.
I work for you, Mister Andersen. Your pie. Your plate.
But you still save me a slice every time.
Your newspaper miss a page.

The front page was a story about a fire. A sawmill that employed Chinese men.
Since when you read Chinese?

It's what everyone was talking about. I didn't want you to worry.

You did not want me to worry.

Our daughters grew up together. You're like family. I just want you to know that I will use all my power to protect you and your family, no matter what.

Okay.

Good night,
Miss Andersen!
晚安,Mei!

SMACK!

Join us,
Mei! We're telling
stories!

Everyone in camp knows that I tell the best stories.

Ooh, I love your stories. Tell a story, Mei!

You know I was born in Reno, right? I've never been to China.

Have you heard about Auntie Po, the mother of all loggers?

Yes, of course, I just asked you to tell –

– shhh, this one is a new one...

Probably. Maybe.

Is Pei Pei in this one?

You'll never get a story if you don't stop interrupting.

Does she know Paul Bunyan?

I don't know, but Paul Bunyan sure knows about Auntie Po. Everyone knows about Po Pan Yin.

Po Pan Yin stood taller than the tallest white pine, and she cut them down too.

With her loyal blue buffalo Pei Pei, Auntie Po ran the most efficient logging crew west of the Mississippi and –
Mei, really. Everyone here already knows about Auntie Po.

Oh, but have you heard about the summer of the giant mosquitos?
Oooh, this is a good one.

Ugh, the mosquitos!
They caused a lot of trouble at camp, being so big and bitey.
Auntie Po tended to ignore normal-sized mosquitos, but these were large enough to bite her! Auntie Po hated being itchy.

Auntie Po hated the mosquitos and she decided she would fix that problem.

For that, she relied on her loyal cook, Sourdough Sam. He was her favorite cook and he was the only one who could do it fast enough to feed her whole crew.
Auntie Po had remembered the giant bumblebees from her travels in the Midwest.
She dispatched Sourdough Sam to retrieve a pair of them, hoping to pit their ferocious butt-stingers against the mosquitos.

Sourdough Sam brought them to camp, having flown the bumblebees over mountain ranges and at least two big lakes to get there!
But at camp...well.
Should I tell them the rest, Bee?
I don't know, they're just kids. I don't know if they can take it.
MEI!! Come on!!!!
Please tell us! Please!

Well, it turns out the bumblebees took a liking to the mosquitos.
What kind of liking?
I mean, they really, really liked each other...
Oooooooo...
They mated, and produced a terrifying hybrid of mosquito bees!
Beequitos? Mosquibees?
They had mouth-stingers AND butt-stingers!
BUTT-STINGERS!

Oh nooooo!
Butt-stingers to sting you in the butts!
Language, Polly.
Language, Henry.
Winnie!!! Winnieeee! Winnie!!

I'm by the fire, Pauly!

My beautiful wife!
My not very beautiful sister!
Come on, let's get you home.
Give me a kiss, Winnie! We cut a thousand trees today. We'll have the forest cleared by first snowmelt!
Yes, dear.
See that, Bee? That's how to be a good wife.

Maybe if you wore a better dress? I dunno, your hair's not great either.

Mei doesn't even wear dresses, and she is very pretty.

No one cares who Mei marries. Isn't that right, Mei?
Don't talk to Mei like that.

She's not like us, Bee.
Mei doesn't have a real future.

You're an awful pig, Pauly!

Bee says that I feel more things than she does, but maybe it's because more things happen to me than happen to her.

ARGHHH!

Ugh.

Snorf.

!?

Snerfff.

Snerf.
Wait!!
!!?

MEI!

Oh, I'm so glad to see you!

It was so dark, I wasn't sure I'd find you.
I brought you a coat. It's cold.
Thanks.

Um. Did you see that?

No. See what?

Never mind. I must be hallucinating.

I'm sorry about Pauly. He's just a stupid oaf. Don't listen to him, Mei.
He's not wrong.

You can go to university. You can get married.

I'll probably work in a kitchen my entire life. Maybe I'll become head cook when my father can't anymore, and you and your beautiful children can visit me sometime.

Well, maybe we can go to university together, and live in a darling little boarding house run by a strict matriarch.

And then I'll marry a handsome and brilliant man, and you will too!

This is Bee's story. Bee will go to university, and marry a man.

I don't think I want to get married.

But why?
I don't like boys.

Well, you'll move in with me and you'll write stories and poems under a man's name and sell them to the paper. I'll illustrate them for you.
That...sounds very nice, actually.

You could write romance novels about loggers! Oh, maybe you can open a pie shop and I'll work the register.
A bookstore and pie shop!

I could teach at the orphanage in the morning, and then work the afternoon shift in the pie shop, and then we can walk home and make dinner together!
Your husband might have to get used to late dinners.

Husband?

The handsome and brilliant man you're going to marry?
Oh, right! Maybe he'll run an import business and travel a lot so we won't have to worry about him much.
Hee hee.

I'll have a small but lovely wedding. There'll be dancing and you will be my bridesmaid.
I don't know how to dance.

Oh!

Get up. I'm going to teach you.

I'll be the boy. Put your hand on my shoulder.
Hand in mine.
Follow me.
Where did you learn how to dance?
My dad made me learn. Said I had to be a little bit respectable.

That's why my dad only wanted me to speak English. He said I needed to learn how to be American.

You speak better English than Pauly!

I know!

You are pretty good at dancing.
Can we try a twirl?

EEP!
Whoa!

HAHAHAHAHAHAHA
Are you okay?!

I'll have three children, and they'll call you Auntie Mei.
I will make them so many pies.
They will be the fattest little cream-filled children.
Hee hee hee.
I think we'll be friends forever, Mei.

This is a good story. This is a nice story. This is still Bee's story.

Well, we've come this far.

CHAPTER two

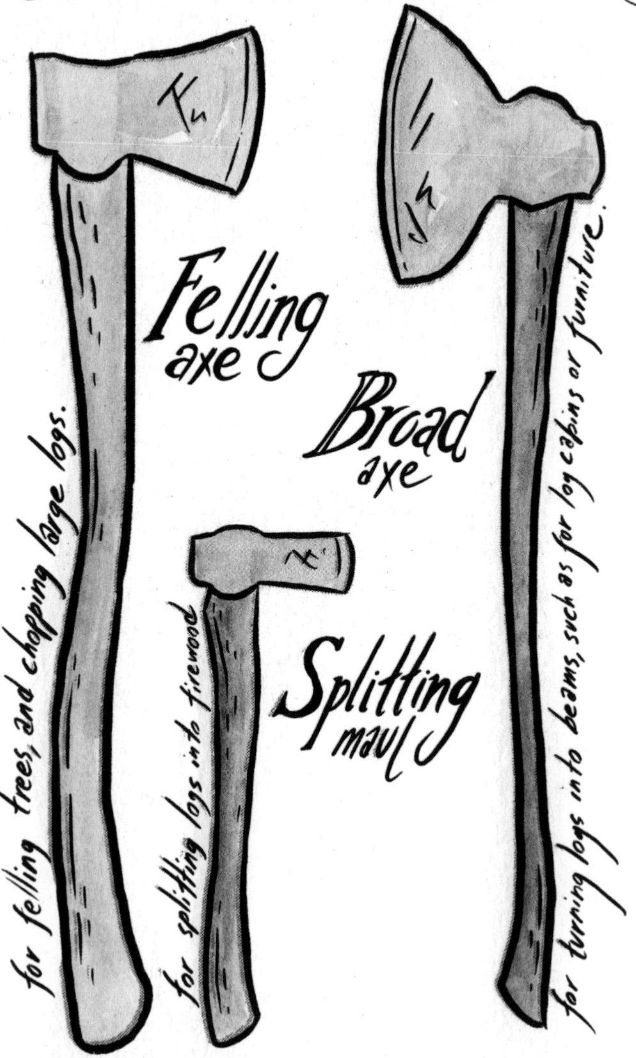

Felling axe

for felling trees, and chopping large logs.

Broad axe

for turning logs into beams, such as for log cabins or furniture.

Splitting maul

for splitting logs into firewood

It's halfway through the season, brother. I can only give you a job in the kitchen.
Great, I'll get those Chinamen into shape!
You know, I was a great head cook before I started getting in fights!
Neils. You were getting in fights before you learned to walk.
Besides, I already have a head cook. Hao is excellent.
The scrawny Chinaman?!
He is very strong for his size.

A Chinaman can't make schnitzel.

His schnitzel is magnificent. He uses Doreen's recipe.

Doreen. The best thing that ever happened to you.

Take my wife's name out of your mouth.

Pah! It is no wonder she left you. You have your daughter running around in the kitchen with Chinamen and scoundrels.

It is none of your business how I raise Beatrice.

You know I can cook better than this Hao.

No, you can't. Do you want a job or not?

...yes.

Report to the kitchen at dawn tomorrow, then. Hao will tell you what to do.

PAH!

Did you hear all that?

Inventory and budget, Mister Andersen.

This isn't your writing.
It is better!
I teach Mei how to manage kitchen! But this is first week she did it herself.
She's a natural.
Beatrice tells me she is a very good writer. And the kids love her stories.
Thank you! Miss Andersen has help with her reading.

I'm sure that was true when our girls were kids. But I saw Mei with *Pride and Prejudice* the other day.
The storybook with the talkative girl and grumpy man? Eh, I never read it.
Hao. I've never read any of those books either. You have raised a wonderful girl.
Haha, our daughters read more book than us!

I am sorry about Neils. Can you handle him?
I handle two month sleeping in boat!
I handle fifty pound of potato every six hour!
Neils is just big loud man.
I can handle.

Logging a forest is like a dance.

The loggers slide past each other,
and sharp blades and soft humans
and heavy logs jostle for space.

Pauly's a boor, but he is good at his job.

Do you ever wish you could work out there with them?
Hmm. It's very dangerous.
Mmm-hmm.
Bee, are you listening to me?
Mmmm, yeah?

What are you even looking at?

Oh...who. Who are you looking at?

The new boy.

He just came down from Wisconsin, and he's from a logging family just like me.

Dad says that he's a natural leader. He's young, but the men trust him!

Dad says he'll be a foreman in two or three years.

If he doesn't die first.

Mei!

You said it's a dangerous job!
What's gotten into you?!
I'm going for a walk. I need to get kindling for the stoves.
I can go with you!
No, thanks.

Why do I feel so bad!
Bee is just confiding in me about normal girl things.
And I should like that.
I don't like it!!!

KICK
Ugh.
AUGHHH.

!!!
AAAAAAAAAAAAAA!!!
...

AAAAAAAAAAAAAAHHH

I hear you've been telling stories about me.
Yes! But I made you up! You're just a story.
Wait, I can make things real with my brain?
Be careful, Ah Mei. It will be difficult.
Um, okay. You didn't answer my question. Wait, what do I need to be careful of?

Wait!
I have questions!

Aughhh, even the gods I invent aren't that useful.
!

I wish Bee could see this.

rummage
??

?!

!!!

Th...thank you.

I'll be back, Auntie Po. I have to go make dinner.

SCRATCH SCRATCH

lick

Martha, can you chop? Ah Sam is not back from town.
Of course, Mr. Hao.

Sam is never late, is he okay?
I don't know.

You sent him off to town with two workers and the best horse. I'm sure he's fine.

Ham!

Stew!

I didn't make pie today! But Bee, I have to tell you –

Mei, I didn't come here for pie. You and your dad need to come right now. It's Sam.

Uncle!
There is BLOOD everywhere! You are covered in blood!

It's a head wound. They bleed a lot.
Here, let me. I'm better at this.

We talk outside.

What happen?
They were attacked in town. A bunch of no-good roustabouts trying to drive Chinamen out of town.
Drive Chinamen out of town? I only send Ah Sam to Chinese Camp!
I know, it's not safe there either –
You say we are like family, Mister Andersen?
You are, I am so sorry, I didn't know.
I mean, I knew, but I –
But you cannot stop. You cannot make it safe for my family.

If you cannot
keep us safe, you cannot
call us family!

我沒事
不用担心
I'm fine!
He'll be
okay, Mei.

Henry, you should be inside now.
Is Sam going to be okay?
He's only hurt a little. Your dad helped to stop the bleeding. Thank him, all right?
Mama says it might not be safe for us, either.

Are we going to be okay?
I don't know, Henry.

huff
AUNTIE!
I am talking to you!!
Do you know what happened to Ah Sam? They hit him, and he's my friend!

Oh no, I fell asleep!
Ugh, I smell like a wet buffalo.
Pei Pei?
!!!!!!!!!!

Ah Mei!!
I know! I'm in trouble! You're not my father!

CREAK

Where you go?! Why make me worry?!

Papa, I'm sorry! I fell asleep in the woods, and you'll never believe this, but you know the Auntie Po stories I tell? She's real! So is Pei Pei!

I know you're going to say that I'm just dreaming.

No, no.

Is okay. Just don't fell.

You don't want me to tell Bee about the GIANT AUNTIE and her HUGE WATER BUFFALO?

Mei, sometimes, they can't see same thing.

We are different. You are special girl.

Go and pai pai.

Dear Ah Yeh and Ah Mah, who I never met and never will, please protect my family anyway.
And please help me pull off this really great plan that is going to be so good once my dad stops lecturing me and lets me go get Bee.

Bee, I need your help!

Mei, where were you?! Your father was worried sick, but I figured you just ran to the woods, so I covered for you BUT I don't think it worked. Did you sleep in the forest? You have so many pine needles in your hair!

What kind of idea?

We're going to build a giant buffalo.
Mei, we don't know how to build a giant buffalo.

Not yet! But we will. First, let's make some egg tarts, because we're going to need help.

Uncle Tong!
唐叔叔
小妹妹
Mei mei!
你好,
Miss Andersen!
Lay ho to you too!
We need your help, so Mei brought you a bribe.
Ohhhhh, Mei is good cook.
I know you like my egg tarts the best!

wood stump?
buffalo hog?

How are your families?

My kids are smart! They all go to school.
我孩了很聪、明
他们有上学读书

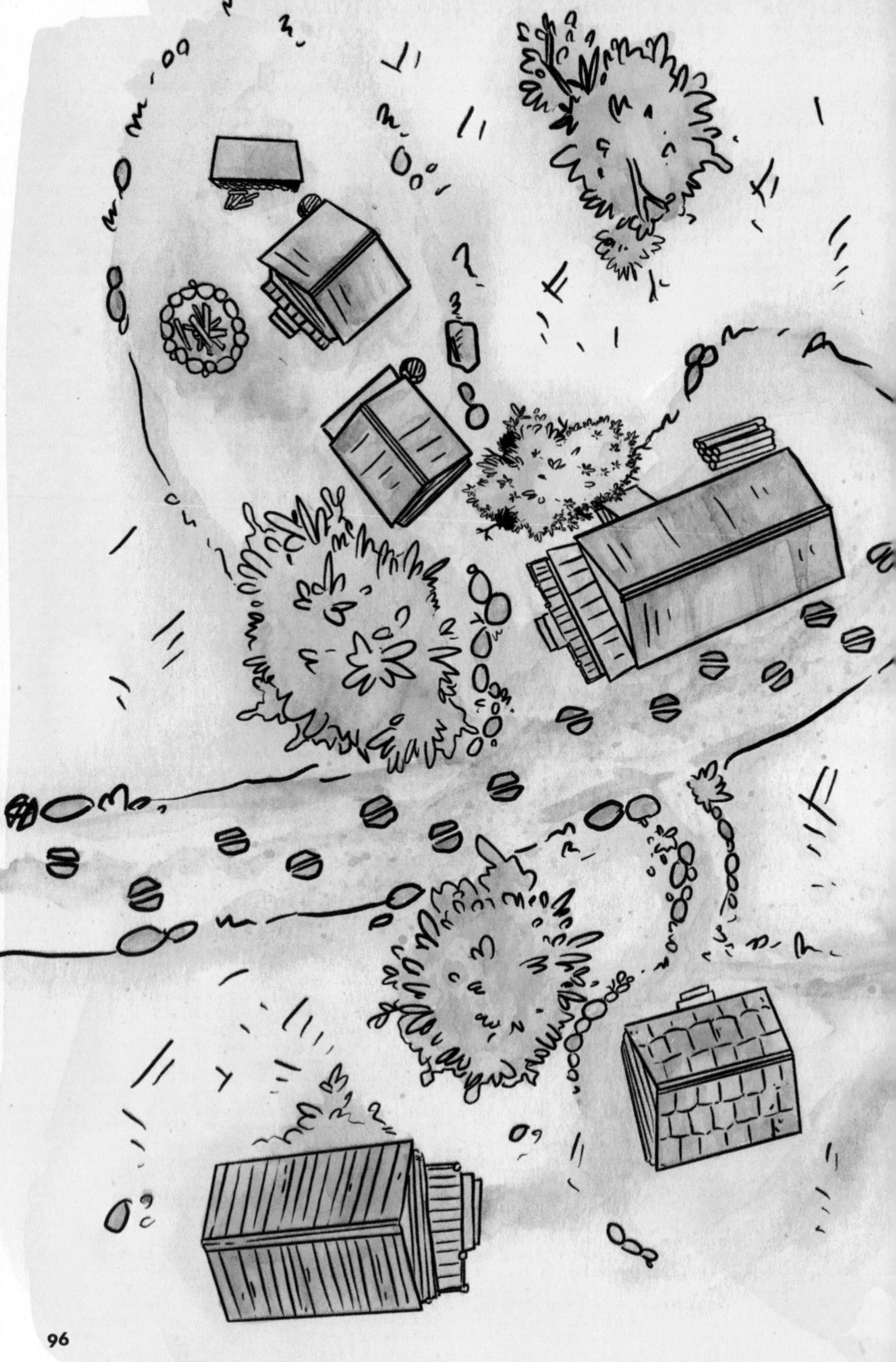

I can stand, you know.
I'm sure you can, but my dad wants you to rest up.

You shouldn't even be peeling potatoes.

Aiyaaaaa!

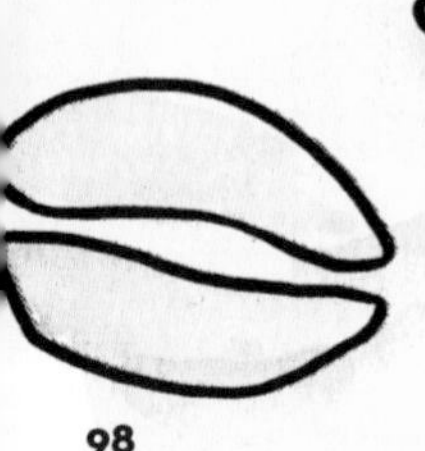

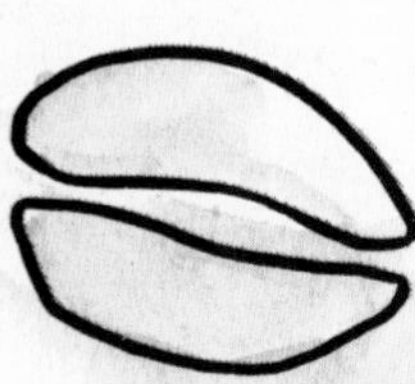

Whoa!
!!!
Whoa.
MEI!
BEEEEEE!!!

He's real! Pei Pei is real!

He'll take care of us, Mama! He's a giant buffalo! He's blue.

We just wanted to make the kids happy.

I wanted them to feel safe and comfortable. Like someone's looking out for them.
You have a good heart.

But you're both old enough to know that it isn't really safe. Not for Mei's family, and not for mine.

But Henry's smiling. Thank you.

CHAPTER THREE

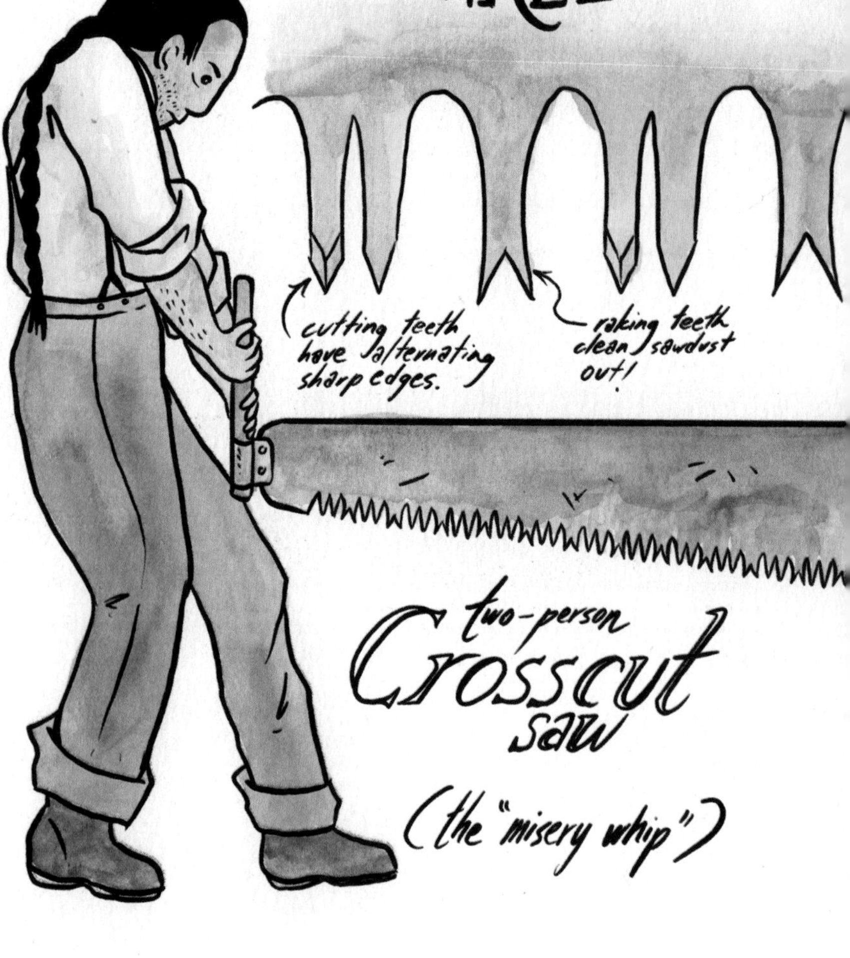

Crosscut saws

are used to cut wood against the grain of the wood.

these saws are used to cut down large trees.

I've set you and Ah Sam up at a boarding house in Chinatown. The first month is already paid, and there is work in town.

The other Chinese workers can stay at camp for now – no one else wants to do that work in the winter – but they'll have to find work at the mines after the season.

I know a restaurant owner that is hiring staff – he needs a few good cooks and he knows you and he wants to hire you. Yee, at the Horseshoe. Tell him Hels sent you.

I know Yee. I don't need introduction.

Do you want Mei to stay with Bee? She can move into Bee's room. I think she'll be safer here with us, and you can visit anytime. You can come with our delivery wagon.

This is the safest thing, for both our families.

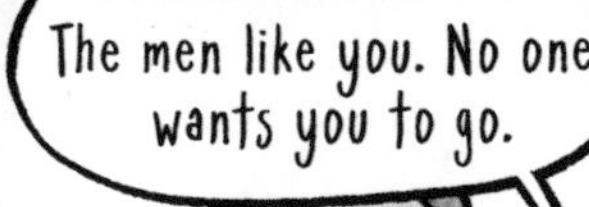
The men like you. No one wants you to go.

Just – they'll make me shut down the camp. Or worse, they'll burn it, like the sawmill. The company is willing to fire my entire crew.

I have a hundred men. And the families. And Beatrice and Winnie and Polly. I have to protect Bee.

Hao, I am so sorry.

Please say something.

Okay, Mister Andersen.

I'll take care of Mei. Bee and her are such good friends.
She's like my own daughter.

She is MY daughter, Mister Andersen.

Please stay in town. I will get this sorted out. This is just politics. You'll be back here in no time.
I will not hold my breathing, Mister Anderson.

Mister Hao.
Mister Andersen.

I'm so sorry, Hao.

Am I...am I head cook now?
There are two German cooks coming in tonight. I want your inventory report every Sunday.

Yes, Hels.
You look nervous.

Mister Hao...is a very good cook.

Yes, he is.

This is temporary, Hao. The tension in town will blow over soon and we'll go back to normal.
This IS normal, Mister Andersen.
Be a good girl.

Are you okay?
I'm fine.

If you want to talk –
What's there to talk about?

This isn't going to stop happening, Bee. Not for me.

My dad said he spent weeks on a boat to come here. He said my life will be better than his. He said we are a people that endure.

Does your family have to endure too, or is it just us?

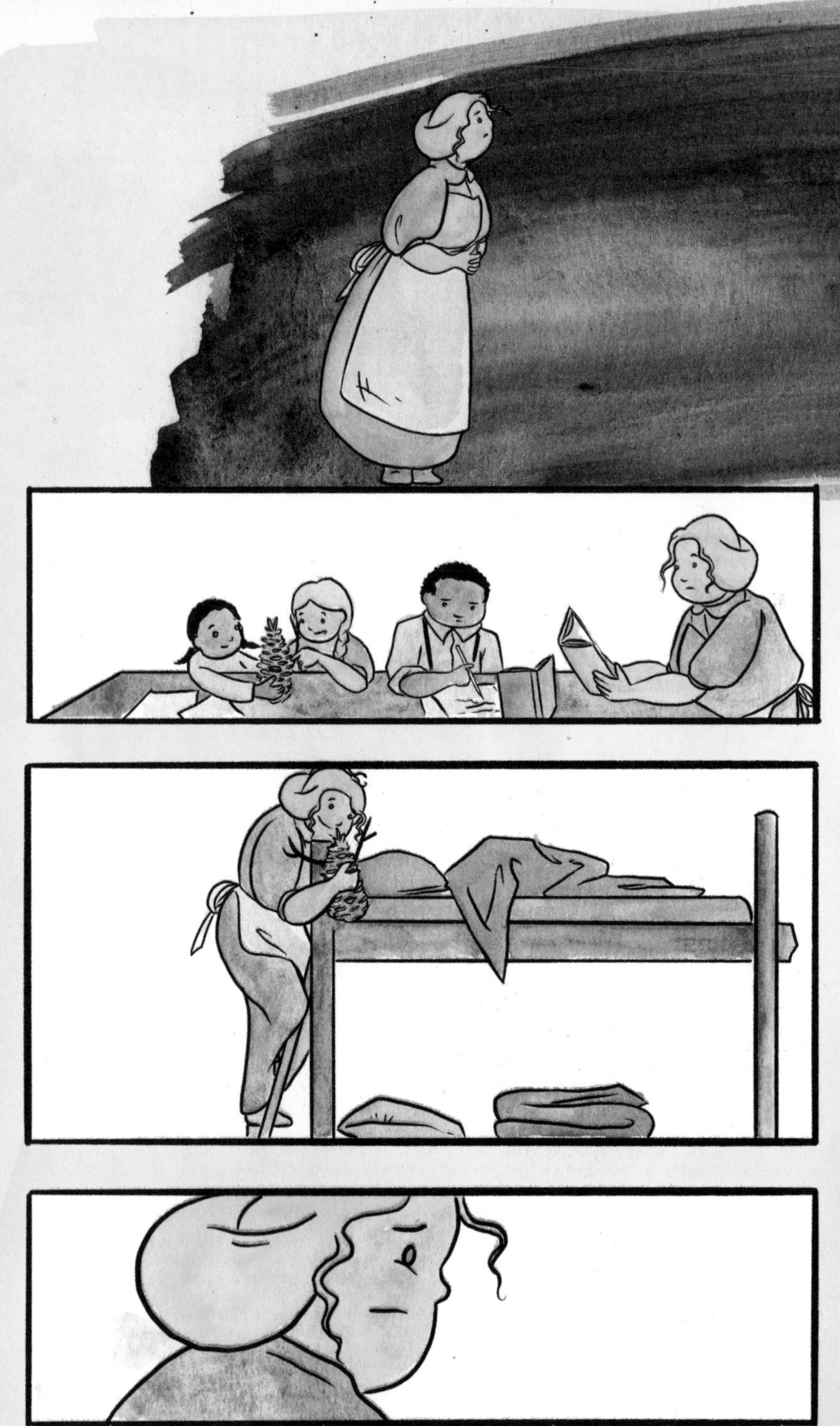

It's been a few weeks. I visit my father on Sundays.

Your father is cutting down a tree by hand, for no good reason.

I can't sleep, Bee.

Shhhh.

Can you tell me a story, Mei?

Let Mei sleep, Polly!

Auntie Po wasn't always the nicest crew chief, but she always tried to protect her crew.
Once, after delivering their load of wood for the season, an entire forest's worth, the sawmill told Auntie Po and her men that they would only pay them half of what they promised. And then the sawmill fired them all!

Auntie Po didn't need the money, but her crew did. They had families!
Auntie Po wouldn't have it, though. She sat outside the sawmill, and she sucked in all the air.
And then, she blew into the river.

All the logs went flowing back upstream, where they piled up around a bend in the river.
Auntie Po sat on the giant pile of logs, a whole forest's worth, and yelled so the entire town could hear.

THE SAWMILL OWNERS ARE CHEATS!
FAIR PAY FOR FAIR WORK!
YOU CAN'T JUST FIRE US!
Mei, you're scaring Polly.

snoreeeeeeee
ZZZZZZZZZZZZZZZZZZZZZZZZ
Never mind.
Thanks.

I'm glad you're using these stories to help express your emotions.
What gave it away?
The screaming, mostly.

The winter passes. I am still angry, but I don't think I'm angry at Bee.

I'm angry that I have to make my own gods.

I'm angry that even the gods I make can't help my family.

I have two forks in my hiding stump!

Why do you have two forks – why do you have a hiding stump?

I also have three spoons and a knife.
Ugh. I wish I had more pockets.

I think this used to be a slug?

YUCK
PTHOEEY !!!
What did they put in this!?
A slug?
Mei! All the loggers will quit if they eat this pie.
I feel like that is not my problem right now.

Thanks for trying to bring me pie, though.

I'm cooking for the Chinese workers that are still at camp. Do you want to help me?

I love helping you.
What are... these ingredients?
Kitchen leftovers. Your uncle is bad at meal planning.
How do you slice them so thin?
Oh, I'll show you.
Hold your knife like this.

Here.
Like this. Cut
slowly.
I think
I'm doing
it!
You're the
fastest learner
I know.
!

!
Um. I should...
Er, I need to...
What was I chopping? I should chop that thing.
Mei. Are you okay?
Of course I'm okay! Ginger! There it is!

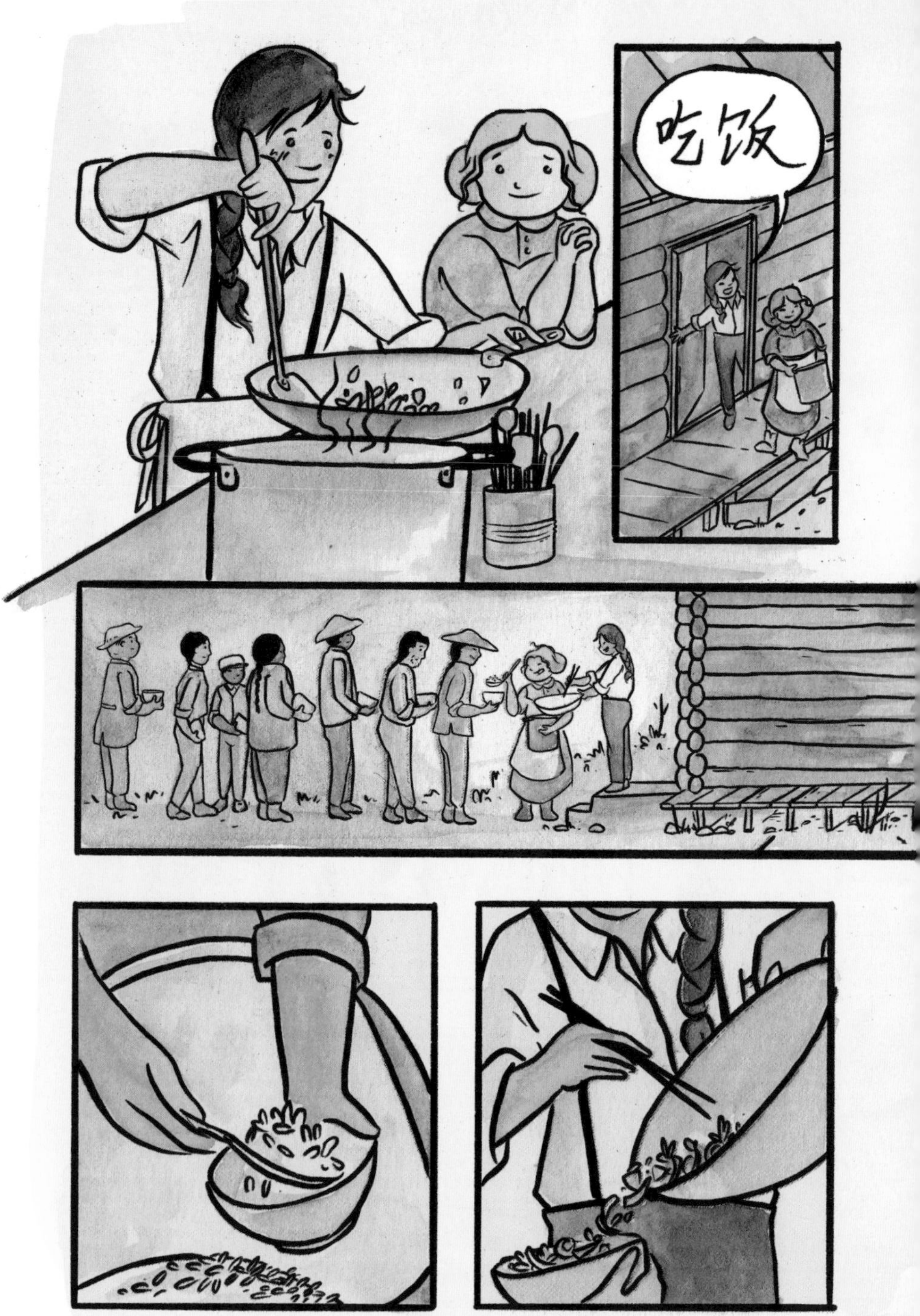

吃饭

This looks delicious!

Hmm, what is this?

Chop suey. Rice and leftovers tossed around in a wok.

Papa picked it up when he was cooking at the railroad.

I can do better if you want to sneak me stuff from the kitchen.

Why are you holding all those fishes?

Why...would I want to help you?

You don't have to. You can hate me and I'll deserve it. But my crew is starving.

We snuck these things out of the kitchen for you.
Neils tried to make schnitzel tonight. From my mother's recipe! She's never been so disrespected.

I wonder if this is what being a god feels like.

Pauly?

Anything, Mei.

Take half your men and peel the potatoes.

Yes! Thank you, Mei!

Hal, can you start a cooking fire? We'll roast the fishes there.
Gladly.

Everyone else, please clean your shoes and follow Bee inside! You're going to chop some vegetables!

If you bring enough ingredients to feed the Chinese workers, I can feed you too.
You have a deal.
You can't feed all the crews by yourself, though. We're going to have a real problem on our hands soon.

Men, please. I can fix this.
Well, turns out Pauly was finally right about something.
We can't work like this! Not with this food!
This is the worst camp food I've ever had to suffer through!
Your own son goes to beg the Chinese girl every night for food! He won't even eat here!
He does?

No work for bad food!
NO WORK FOR BAD FOOD! BOOOOO!

You call this a pie?

SPLAT

I would...not.

NO WORK FOR BAD FOOD! NO WORK FOR BAD FOOD!

That's not a catchy chant, but it does get the point across.
CHONK
CHONK
THUNK
THONK

Have you been going to Mei for food too?
Yes.
I have to talk to Neils.

THEY MOCK MY SCHNITZEL!!!
THEY MOCK MY PIE!
Neils, we have to talk.
No! I quit! And I'm taking the Germans with me!

MEI-
-PAPA
I was going to fire them too, anyway.

BEANS?
MEI-
SAVE PIE FOR MISTER ANDERSEN.
-PAPA
Hey, Dad.

We heard about Neils.
Everyone heard.

I'm sorry to say
this, sir. But you created
this bad situation.

And you know how
to fix this.

I do.
I'm going to
Chinatown.

When you've finished, come back and peel potatoes with me.
I'll go tell the men that you'll be fixing the kitchen problem.
Yes, ma'am!
Go and get my dad back, then. Martha and I can run the kitchen for today's dinner.

I know you can. Thank you.

HORS

HO

SESHOE

...
knock
knock

!
牛柳
Beef tenderloin!

快快
Faster!
Ah Hao...

我很忙
I'm very busy!

Mister Andersen is here.

I know. You want me to come back to cook. My shift here end in thirty minute. You wait.

I was wrong to fire you. I don't care what the company says.

I don't have any crew without you running my kitchen. I'm not afraid of any boycott.

I also want you to come back as my friend, Hao.

Pay me what you pay Neils.

Hao, you don't want that. I only paid Neils half of what you were paid.

Oh.

You're twice the man he is.
Sorry about your crew.
药房
HARMACY

No one can run the kitchen like you do, Hao. Maybe Mei in a few years, but she is still so young.
She shouldn't even be in kitchen.
I agree, she shouldn't. What do you want?
Okay. We can talk.
HORSESHOE

When I work on railroad, we cook big feast for Chinese New Year.
I didn't know it was different.
You never ask.
From now on, I want to cook Chinese New Year dinner for camp.
Of course.

That was easy one.

I already said you could have anything, Hao.

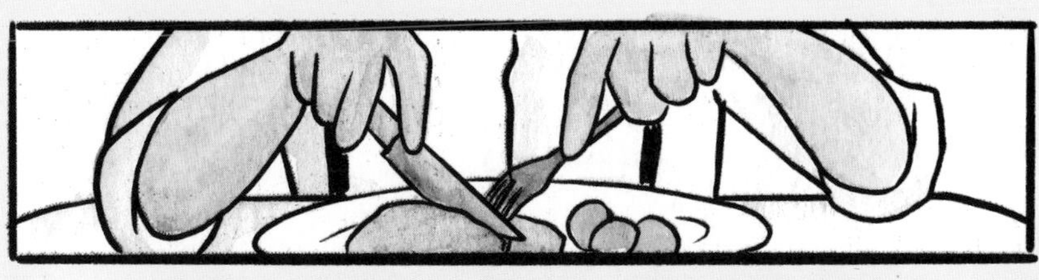

I want one more thing.

All Chinese workers get board. They work same, they eat same.
Done.
They eat same time. Same table.
Our dining hall isn't big enough–
All right. We'll build more tables.

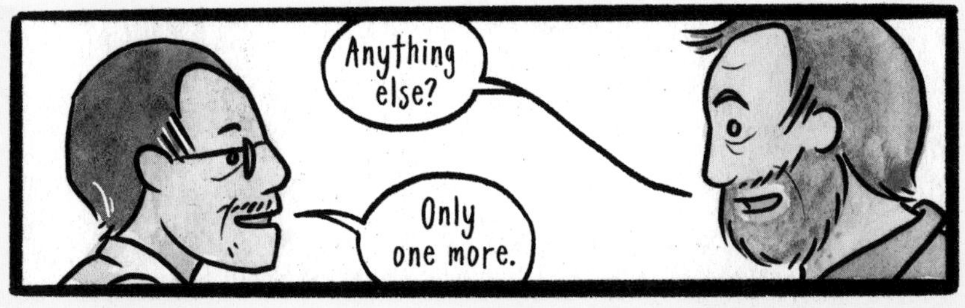
Anything else?
Only one more.

Mei. She want a pony.
Mei wants a pony?

Well, I know a farm that just had a few new foals. If it's trained as a work horse...

SNICKER

HA HAH
HAHAHAA
HAHAHA

HAHAHAHAHAHAHAHAHA
I joke.
hehehehehe

Welcome back, Mister Hao.
HORSE
药房
PHARMACY

the
Jam pike
is a steel spike used to pry logs apart.
the
Cant hook
is a movable steel hook used to grab and roll logs.

CHAPTER four

Auntie Po worked a piece of land shaped like a pyramid, which meant that she could cut down more trees than any other logging crew. But the trees still need to become useful lumber!

So, in the late winter, when the snow begins to melt, Auntie Po starts her log drive.
The workers push the winter's harvest of logs into the cold river.
And the long journey to the sawmill begins.

The logs are guided by the best and bravest workers, the river pigs.
CAMP
downstream
Many camps use flumes to transport logs, and even trains! But the nearest flume is miles away, and the railroad doesn't run near our camp.
SAWMILL
FLUME
But the Andersen family knows log driving from their Wisconsin days, and they're going to show us all how it's done!

The river pigs that worked on Auntie Po's crew had to be stronger and braver than all the others.

It's their job to make sure the logs don't pile up, causing a log jam. A log jam can take hours to clear.

You see, log drives are the most dangerous part of a logger's job.

They have to have good balance to stay upright.
And fast instincts, to navigate the moving logs.

The river is wild and fast.

The river doesn't care about any man.

Of course, Auntie Po's river pigs could jump across half the river in a single bound! They never ever fell.

They could clear log jams with a single push.

But for the biggest log jams, they used dynamite!

And her loyal camp cooks had to follow the log drive down the river.
Even though it was really cold and Auntie Po's men eat way too much food and are also very messy.
Ahem.

Most importantly, Auntie Po never lost a crew member.

Even on the most dangerous log drives, Auntie Po always brought everybody home at the end of the day.

Are you ready to hear about Auntie Po's Round River Drive?
Mei! We load lunch wagon now, and your papa say to come help!

How is your auntie?
Who?

Your Auntie Po.

You... believe me?
!

If you believe, I believe.

Do you see her?

I don't need to see Auntie Po. I know who I am. I am good cook. I have good job. I have good daughter.

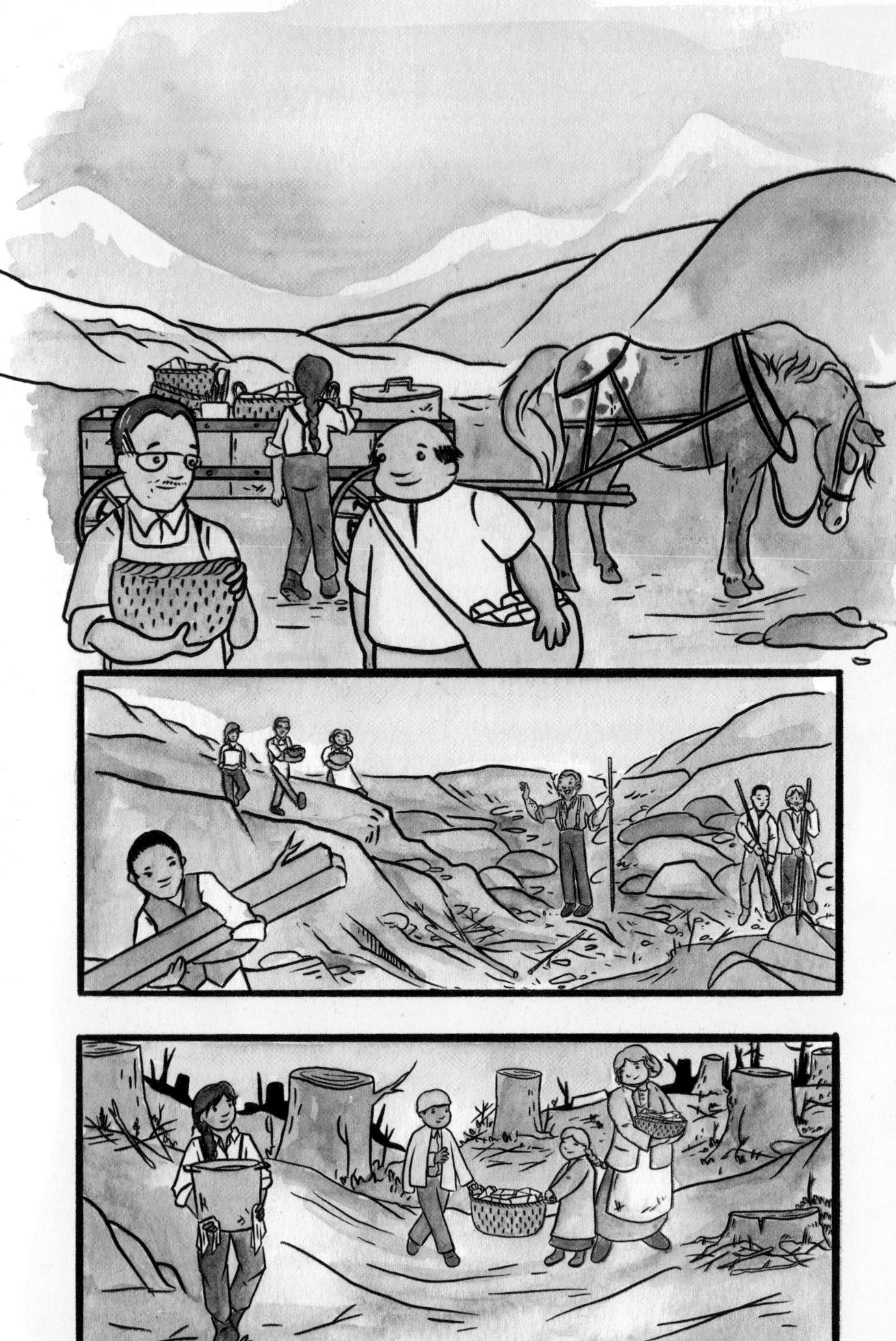

Look at them!

This one for your papa. Special sandwich.
Pa has a special sandwich?

No mustard.
Huh, I didn't know that.

STOP!

Log jam!!

This log jam is pretty bad. You sure you can handle this? We haven't done a real log drive in years, and most of the boys are still green.
Yeah, we can do this. But we're gonna need dynamite, boss.

Well, get your crew ready.
I got it.
Please be careful, son.

Clear out!
Yessir!

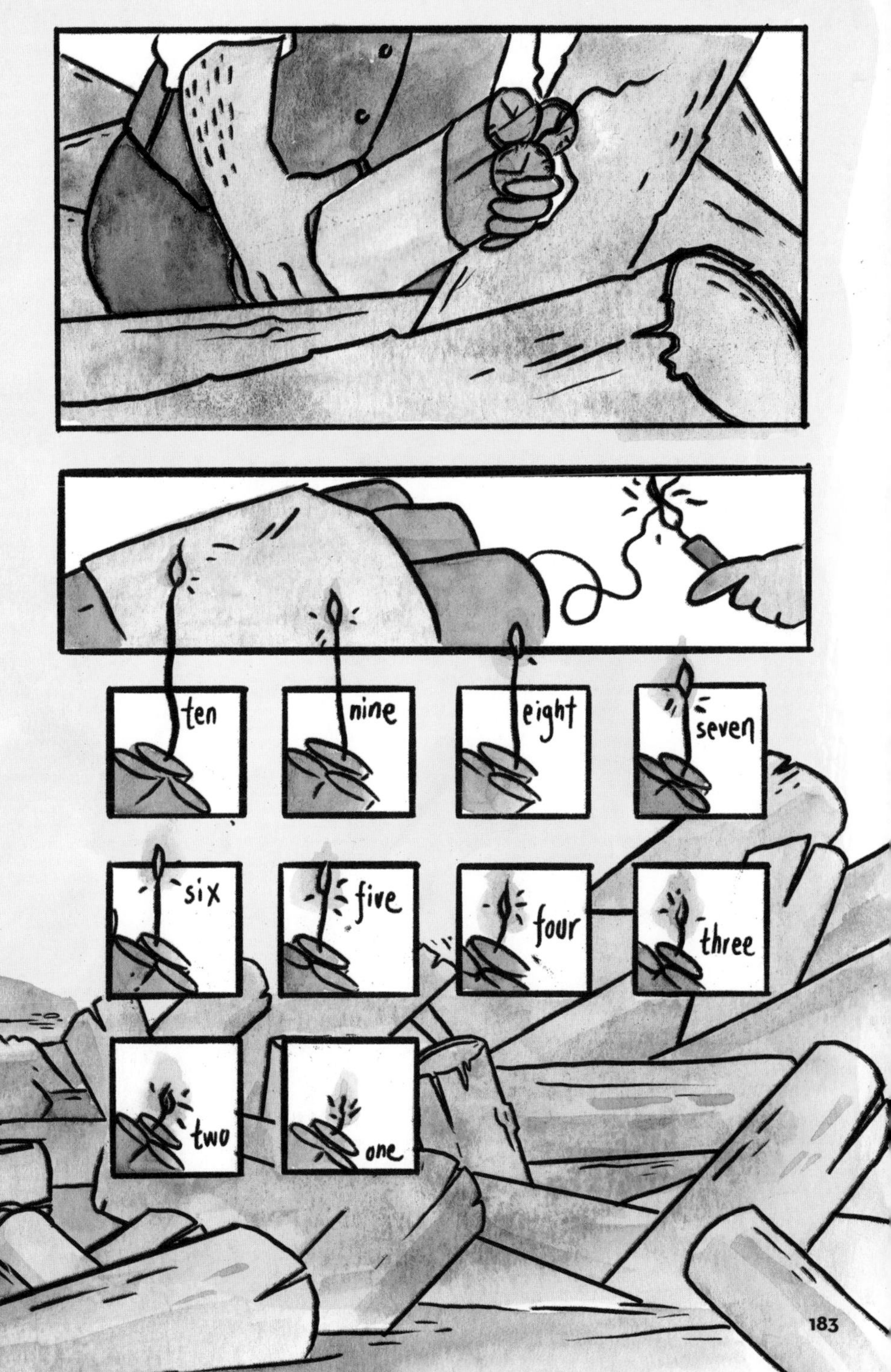
ten
nine
eight
seven
six
five
four
three
two
one

BO

Hal!
Pauly!
!
!?
Oh no.

Please don't let them watch.
Come here, come here.

Auntie Po will save them, right?

Yes, yes. Close your eye, Ah Mei tell you.

Yes, just keep your eyes closed and I'll tell you what's going on.
Listen only to my voice, okay?
I see her, up the river! She's running, leaping over the trees to come to us. She hears us.

Pei Pei is there too.
Of course! She'll need Pei Pei to help move the logs.

She is in
the river now.

She is searching for our men.
The logs are so heavy, but she is so strong.

She is trying so hard.
She'll never stop trying to help us.
She'll work until her hands crack.

She'll work until her back hurts so much she can't stand up.
He jumped right in to help. Don't let him go back in.
You can't swim!
She'll help us even if we don't believe in her.
I have Sam. Go.
Because we're her family.

Hels, watch out!

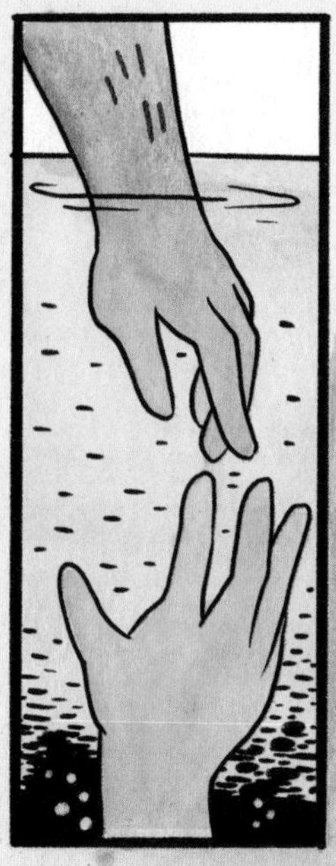

Will she save my dad?
I don't know yet.
I don't know.
Henry!
Oh.

I see her, Mei!

I see her too, Henry.
This is not the time, Mei.

Bee, you really don't see Auntie Po at all, do you?

No, Mei! I don't see Auntie Po!

I see the Chinese workers pulling people out of the water! I see my dad and Hal going back in to help people, over and over! I see your dad and Ah Sam, taking care of everyone.

I don't see pretend gods!

Is everyone out?
COUGH! COUGH!
Wait -
Pauly!

Bee, we need to get the kids back to camp.
Where is my brother?
PAULY!

Pauly is not out yet.
Come, come. We must go.

PAULY!!!
PAPA!!!

Papa...where's Pauly?

Mei.

AUNTIE!!
Auntie?

Why didn't you save Pauly!?

Mei Mei. He was already gone when the logs fell.
Look, Mei. The trees are almost gone. And I have to go soon.

What does that mean?

It means that you don't answer all wishes.

It means you won't save us.

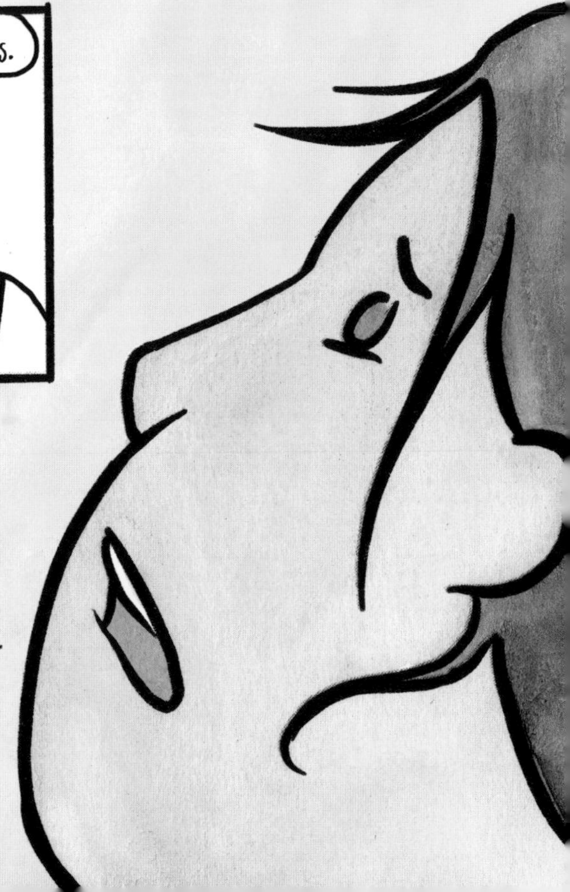
And we're still okay. I'm still okay and I don't need you.

I saw it, I saw it with my own eyes. She stood as tall as the tallest white pine!

She saved my dad.

She just reached right in, and pulled out Mister Andersen with her own hands.

Hey.

She didn't save my brother, Mei.

Your fancy little stories couldn't save my brother.

What good is a god that plays favorites?!

You don't have to pretend she's real, Bee. I know you never could see her.

Oh.

sob

Thank you for being here, Mei.

The work continues almost immediately. Hal leads the rest of the log drive, and then the logs are herded into a flume by the Chinese workers, for transport to the mill.
Mister Andersen takes a small group out to continue the search.

We find Pauly on the third day.

AUGHOW

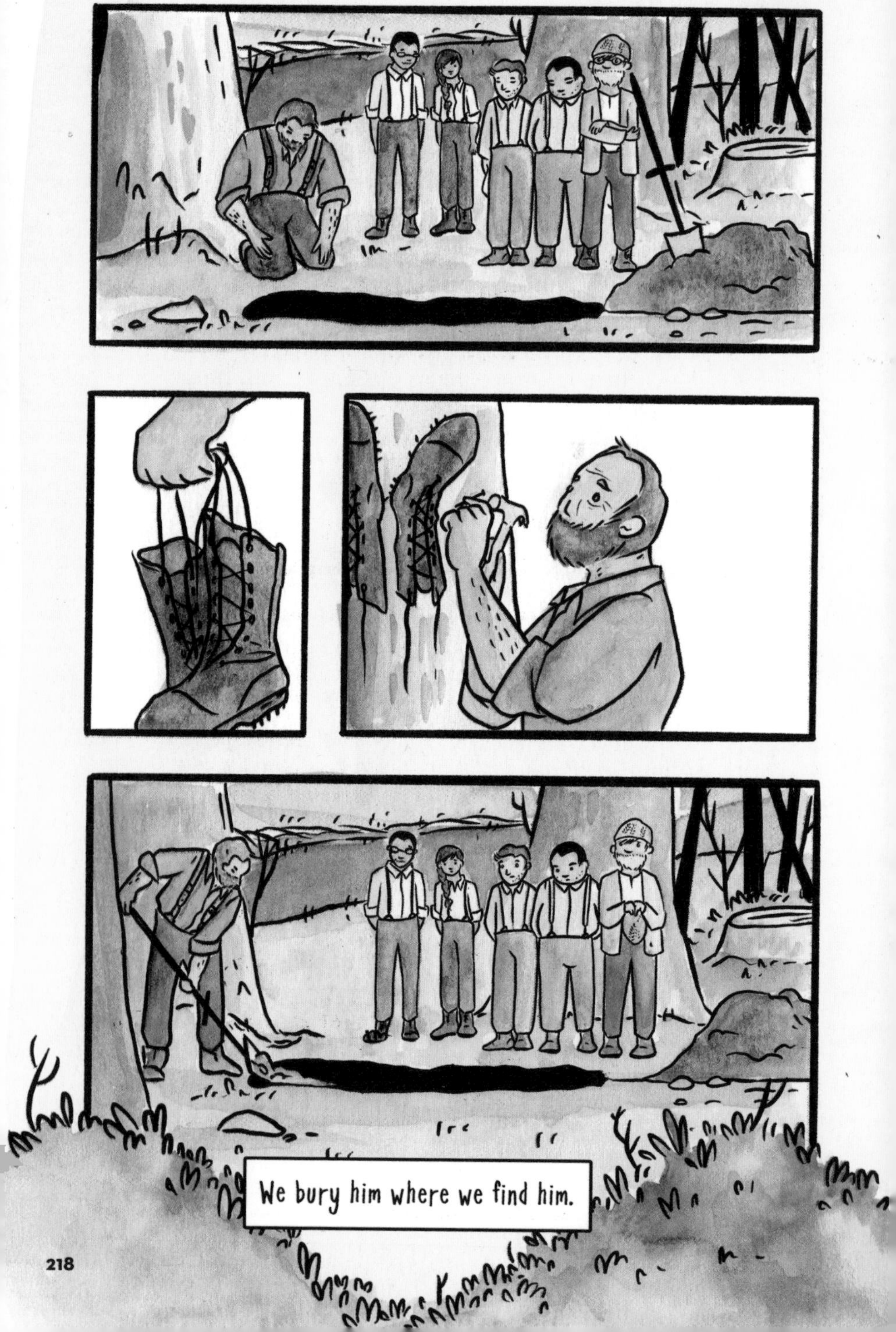

We bury him where we find him.

What is that?

It's a sealed wax bottle with Pauly's name, birthday, and birthplace in it. In case he is found someday.
We use to do in railroad. When we...

When they buried friends by the railroad tracks.

Thank you.

Back to work, boys.

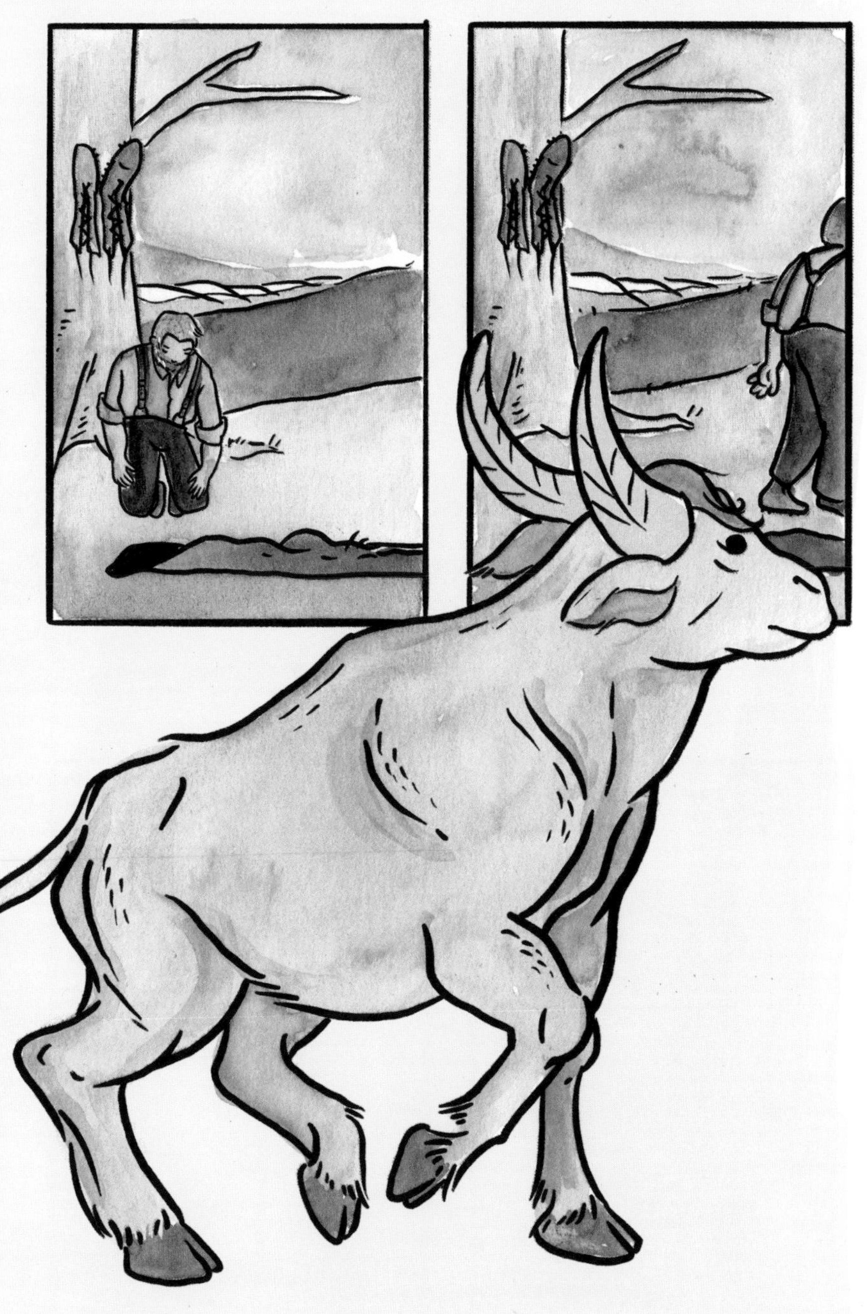

CHAPTER
five
chimney
warming cabinet
Wood stove
wood logs
are loaded
here
oven

coffee pot
spoon
mandoline
scoop made from a gourd
broom
chopsticks
ladle
wok
butter churn
large stockpot

The work is continuing.

I know. My dad says I can't go out with the wagons anymore.

My brother wasn't a hero, you know.

He didn't die for anything.

He just lived a...normal life.

He just lived. And then he died. And the work didn't stop. The world didn't stop.

I didn't get to see him before he was buried.

I went to his grave to say goodbye. I planted a tree. He never cared about flowers, so it didn't make sense to leave him flowers.

I'm sorry.

It's still warm.

Thanks.

He leaves them tea and rice and oranges sometimes. As an offering. We light incense.

Like they're gods?

No, it's different from that.

I don't either. I've never been to China. I don't think I'll ever meet the rest of my family. I guess I just want to hold on to all the scraps of my family, all these rituals that I don't remember the reasons for.

Do you know what my favorite ritual is?

It's pie, Mei. You bring me pie when I'm sad, and you save me pie when I'm not.

Your dad always saves my dad a slice of pie too.

That's my favorite ritual.

Oh. I think that maybe it's mine too.
Hey, some of the Chinese workers pooled their money. They're going to hold kind of a funeral tonight for Pauly, out of respect for your father.
Do you want to come with me?

Dear friends, we are gather here today, in the sight of a god...
Isn't this from Pauly and Winnie's wedding?
哎呀呀
Aiyaaaa...

Actually, our funeral can be many day and many rules.
But Pauly not Chinese. And he already bury.
I am also cook, not monk.
It is just respect, Sam. This is not for us.
Are all Chinese funerals like this?
I...don't know.
We just want to do something for your family, Bee.
No, no. Please. I appreciate it.
Let us go outside.

What is that?
We buy from Chinatown!
Sometimes, we burn paper versions of the gifts and money we'd like to send to the afterlife.

The paper factory is custom make. Pauly like work, so maybe he can have own wood mill.
Wow, they made a whole wood mill out of paper.
Thank you for all this.

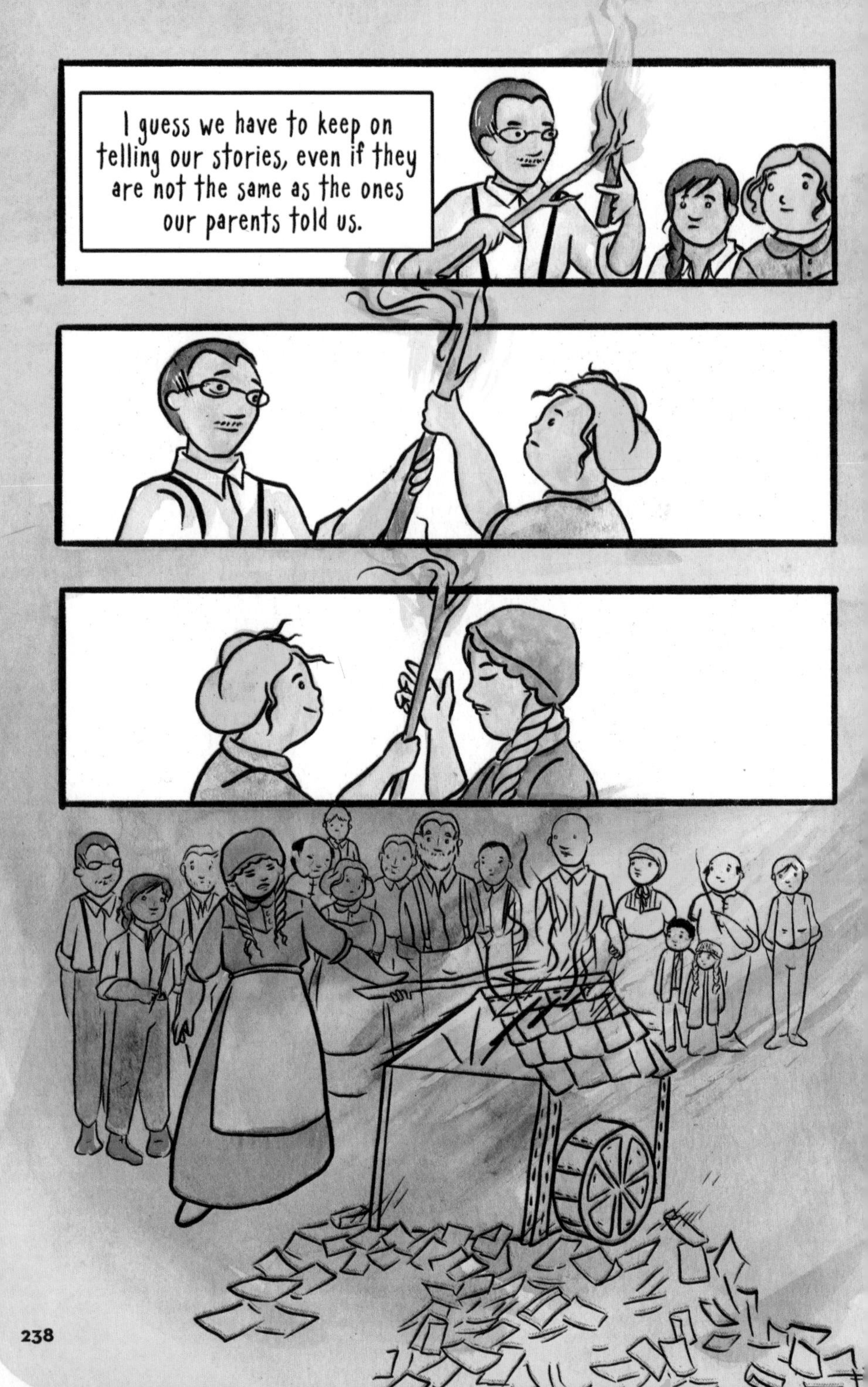
I guess we have to keep on telling our stories, even if they are not the same as the ones our parents told us.

I like it when our stories change when we share them with new people.
I like that their stories will be different.

February 1886, Chinese New Year.

Goodness, where did all these chickens come from?

Thank you, Bee!

谢谢你、

Steam fish!
Dumpling!

Egg tarts, my favorite!
Mr. Hao...how much food did you make?

Lumberjack eat a lot.

To Pauly.
To Pauly! God rest his soul!

To Mister Hao!
To Ah Hao! The best cook in the mountains!
And a happy Chinese New Year!

Happy Chinese New Year!
-clink

恭喜发财
Happy New Year!

恭喜发财

Gong heeey...
...faaat choy?

HAHAHAHAHAHA
They'll get it eventually.

Eat more! Eat more!
I'm so full...

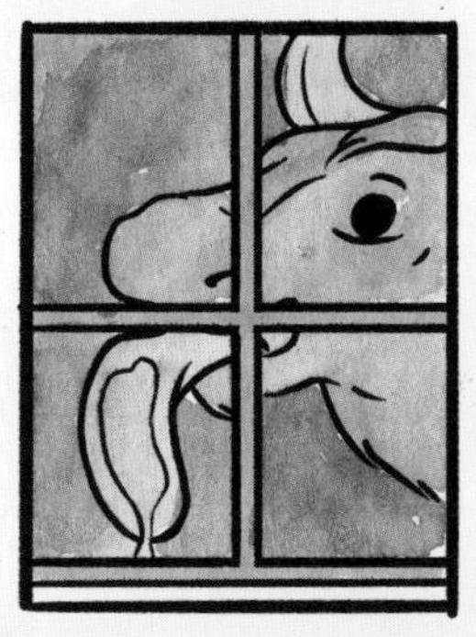

Hao, you've truly outdone yourself!
You like it?
Ah Hao, you did a wonderful job. All of you.
Ah! Thank you, Mister Andersen.
Hao, do you think you can call me Hels?

Yes. I think I can.
Thank you.

Hearls. Helsh?

I think...hard name for American to say.

Maybe you change for good business.

I have something for you. I hope it is okay.

I did some reading, and I asked Yee at the Horseshoe Restaurant if there was anything...

Um. Here.

You give me...
lai see?
红包
It's a tradition, right?

Is Chinese tradition! You're not Chinese!

You give lai see to me!?

Hal and I distributed them to the Chinese crew earlier, but I wanted to give these to you myself.

To health and good fortune!

Mei! Do not open now, not polite!
SMACK

Um. Gong Hey Fat Choy to all of you.

That's pretty close! Thank you, Mister Andersen!

One more thing, Hao. If you don't mind. Can we talk outside?

Next year, I'll be moving to the city. I don't want to work with the company anymore. It was a dream of Pauly and me to start our own family mill. I'm going to start a new mill, Hao. My own mill – and I'll make all the decisions.

Hao, I'd really like you and Mei and Ah Sam to come with me.

Oh.

The new mill will be near Chinatown. It's the biggest one in the whole country.

Okay, we go.

I'm going to make sure the mill is a success. Our success.
Is okay for you if not success. For us, it is different.
But in San Francisco, Mei can go to school.
Also, maybe her Cantonese will get better. It is so bad!

I've another matter to discuss. It's about Mei.
It has come to my attention that Mei has not received proper wages for her kitchen work.
Open it.
! ! !

You cannot give Mei money like that!
It really is just back pay. Maybe she can use it for university in a few years.
How she go to university? Mei is Chinese girl!
Things have been changing in San Francisco.
If Mei wants to go to university, we'll make sure she can go.
Mei can go to university...

Mei can do...anything she want.
Yep.
Sometimes, we talk about starting pie shop. Hao Family Pie Shop.
I promise I'll do everything to help you make that happen.

Maybe you better not make so many promise.

But Mei is smart girl. She will pass all the test.

I have absolutely no doubt that she will.

I think our daughters will get to do all the brilliant things we've never even dared to dream about.

I was going to tell you, you know.

I thought this story was going to be different. But it's still a good story.

Sometimes, our stories have to end, so we can have more of them. I like this story anyway.
!
I am very happy for you, Bee.
I know you wanted more.
What do you want, Mei?

Sometimes, we won't always get everything we want. But the things I can have – well, they're still very good.

I want us to be friends forever.
We'll be friends forever.

I want us to live marvelous lives, that we can tell each other about every time we see each other again.

This is my story with Bee. But Bee has her story too. And I have my own.
And maybe when you graduate and marry a handsome and rich man, we can open a pie shop together.

I'll
dance at your
wedding.
And we'll
write stories
together!

Did you know about the time I worked on Paul Bunyan's crew, on the Round River?
Pah! Auntie Po's crew did a log drive there and they cut twice as much as Bunyan's men!

And I'll feed
your fat little children
so many pies.

So, we're moving to San Francisco.
Do you think it'll be safer there? For us, and Ah Sam, and everyone?
Mei. I cannot make promise like Mister Andersen make promise.
How do you do it? How do you wake up every day knowing...well, not knowing!
I cook. I cook for you.
You cook for everyone.
Ah Mei, I cook for you.
Do you want to go to university?

What? Yeah, I want to go. I mean, it's still a few years away. Yeah, of course!

But I didn't really think -

Then I fire you.
!

No job. No more work in kitchen. We hire new cook.
Oh.

No more cooking.

Only study now!

Must pass exam for university.

Oh, I'll pass.

Okay.
Maybe you still make pie.
Okay.

You are good girl, Mei.

I try to say, but sometimes I -

Pa. I know. I love you too.

Do you still see your Auntie Po?

Does it matter?

I don't need to. I know who I am. I am a good cook. I have good friends. I have the best pa in the world.

I didn't make that.
I did. Gotta practice, since we'll only have you for a couple more years.
Not bad!
Do you feel all right about Bee heading to Wisconsin?

I do.

I guess for so long, she was my only friend.

And I'd always believed that she was going to leave someday, while I'd be stuck here. Like she had this whole exciting story ahead of her, and my only real option was to someday run this kitchen.

But that's not true, is it?
Of course not.

I can want more too. I'm going to leave for university in a few years, and I'm going to make more friends.
I'm going to meet a lot of other girls.
And I'll still make the best pie for miles.

Do you think this will work?
He loved pies. So I thought I'd try to send him one.
Let's try it!

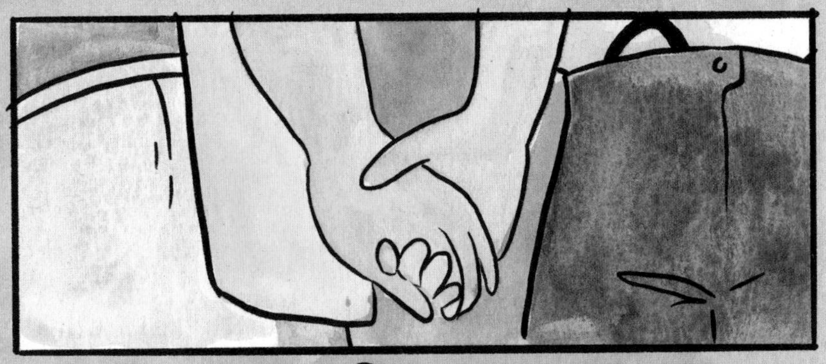

So, she's leaving?

That's what she does, right? That's what we do too. We move camps all the time. When you come to see us next year, we'll be in San Francisco.
I thought that maybe if you asked her to stay –

I didn't want to ask her to stay.

I'll write you every day.
Well, once a week is plenty.

Sometimes my stories are imperfect, but my stories are still real.
I'm going to have my very own story now.

the end

AUTHOR'S NOTE:

When I wrote this book, I was hoping that it would be released in a new era of traditional publishing—one that was a vibrant landscape of stories from all kinds of marginalized voices. I sought to tell a single specific story, a story about one queer Chinese American girl contending with her place in a world that isn't catering to her needs, the tensions and friendships of a marginalized working class navigating proximity to whiteness for both the privilege and violence it confers, and a story about who gets to own a myth. I hope it is read as that specific story.

There are some omissions from this book, the most important being that there are no named Indigenous characters.

The story of Indigenous people and logging camps is complex. Many people were complicit in the erasure of Native Americans from their land, including Black people, and Chinese and European immigrants. This book was written and completed on the traditional lands of the Tongva. The Sierra Nevadas, the area where this book takes place, was historically inhabited by the Yokut, Sierra Miwok, Maidu, Mono, Northern Paiute, Southern Paiute, and Washoe, who still live in the region today. Native Americans worked in logging camps, including in the Sierra Nevadas, and some reservations also operated their own logging concerns. There is documentation of Native American logging camp foremen being valued, as they could communicate with both white people and Indigenous logger crews. There is also documentation of Native Americans being paid less than white immigrants. This is a complicated story and a story that needs nuance, and ultimately, I did not think it was my story to tell. But they were there. We were all there. This history, like all American history, is not a white story.

Researching working class Chinese in lumber camps is not easy. To that end, I am grateful to the scholars and writers whose academic sources I read. Specific details, like Ah Hao being paid more than Neils, and the small glass bottles to mark burials by train tracks, come from the research and writing done by Sue Fawn Chung (*Chinese in the Woods*) and the late Iris Chang (*The Chinese in America*), respectively. Ultimately, where I took liberties with history, I chose to do so because when our histories have been repressed and our people were not deemed worthy enough to document, I feel that we have the obligation to return ourselves to the narrative. If history failed us, fiction will have to restore us.

Thank you.

BIBLIOGRAPHY:

Aarim-Heriot, Najia, and Roger Daniels. *Chinese Immigrants, African Americans, and Racial Anxiety in the United States, 1848–82.* University of Illinois Press, 2003.

Barth, Gunther. *Bitter Strength.* Harvard University Press, 1964.

Chang, Iris. *The Chinese in America.* Penguin, 2004.

Chung, Sue Fawn. *Chinese in the Woods.* University of Illinois Press, 2015.

Chung, Sue Fawn, and Priscilla Wegars. *Chinese American Death Rituals.* AltaMira Press, 2005.

Edmonds, Michael. *Out of the Northwoods.* Wisconsin Historical Society, 2010.

Farquhar, Francis P. *History of the Sierra Nevada.* University of California Press, 2007.

Felton, Harold W. *Legends of Paul Bunyan.* University of Minnesota Press, 2008.

Shephard, Esther. *Paul Bunyan.* New York : Harcourt, Brace, 1924.

Stewart, Bernice, and Homer A. Watts. "Legends of Paul Bunyan, Lumberjack." *The Wisconsin Academy of Sciences, Arts, and Letters*, 1916.

ACKNOWLEDGMENTS:

I am honored to have finished this book in collaboration with, and the primary company of, people of color, who I never ever had to explain myself to. The Kokila team is a dream to work with—I am so grateful to Namrata Tripathi, for shaping and guiding this book with thoughtfulness and a critical eye, to Jasmin Rubero for her visual instinct and excellence, and to Sydnee Monday, Joanna Cárdenas, and Zareen Jaffery for contributing their insight and experience to the book-making process.

My agent, DongWon Song, believed in this book from the very start, and I am grateful for both his counsel and friendship.

My parents were constant cheerleaders, but also actual collaborators in reviewing drafts of my book, and giving me comments, both snarky and useful. Specifically, my mother did and advised on all the Cantonese translations in this book; and the majority of Chinese characters in the book are her own handwriting.

My husband, Jason Bender, is my bedrock, and also a solid beard drawing reference.

Heather Gilbraith, my horse friend, penciled every horse and buffalo in this book, filling in for one of my deepest inadequacies as an artist. If the horse parts still do not fit together correctly, it is entirely my fault; if they do, Heather deserves all the credit.

The book is fictional, but it was written on a fundamental anchor in academic research, specifically Sue Fawn Chung's *Chinese in the Woods* and Iris Chang's *The Chinese in America*. The former is an academic press book which I had trouble finding when I first had the seed of this book in my head; Leigh Walton, who expresses affection with research, sent me a .pdf from the NYPL ten minutes after I complained about not being able to find a hard copy.

The final stages of this book were completed in COVID-19 quarantine, between March and August 2020. For the people who helped to hold my brain together during this period—Leslie Levings, Sarah Gailey, Matthew Marco, Callie Rogers and Eron Rauch, the Monsterhearts crew, the Waywarders, the Space Gnomes, the Space Hobos, the Team DW Slack, my secret Twitter pals, the Comics Campers, the great indoor fighters—thank you; I needed you.

Finally, a thank you to the very good animals I pet while working on this book—Tinkerbell, Alma, Nacho, Precious, Henry, Rufio, Inky, Odin, Pagan, Chelsea, Ginny, and as always, my best friend Bug.